Rosetta's Dress Mess

Rosetta's Dress Mess

WRITTEN BY
LAURA DRISCOLL

ILLUSTRATED BY
DENISE SHIMABUKURO
& THE DISNEY STORYBOOK ARTISTS

RANDOM HOUSE 🏠 NEW YORK

Library of Congress Cataloging-in-Publication Data

Driscoll, Laura.
Rosetta's dress mess / written by Laura Driscoll ; illustrated by Denise
Shimabukuro & The Disney Storybook Artists.
p. cm. — (Disney fairies)
Summary: Garden talent and fashion trendsetter Rosetta is thrilled to be
asked to design a dress for the fairy fashion show, but when she loses her
sense of style, she must ask her less fashionable friends for help.
ISBN 978-0-7364-2854-5 (pbk.)
*[1. Fashion design—Fiction. 2. Ability—Fiction. 3. Friendship—Fiction.
4. Fairies—Fiction.] I. Shimabukuro, Denise, ill. II. Disney Storybook Artists.
III. Title.*
PZ7.D79Ros 2012
[Fic]—dc23   2011021883
randomhouse.com/kids
Printed in the United States of America
10 9 8 7 6 5 4 3

All About Fairies

IF YOU HEAD toward the second star on your right and fly straight on till morning, you'll come to Never Land, a magical island where mermaids play and children never grow up.

When you arrive, you might hear something like the tinkling of little bells. Follow that sound and you'll find Pixie Hollow, the secret heart of Never Land.

A great old maple tree grows in Pixie

Hollow, and in it live hundreds of fairies and sparrow men. Some of them can do water magic, others can fly like the wind, and still others can speak to animals. You see, Pixie Hollow is the Never fairies' kingdom, and each fairy who lives there has a special, extraordinary talent.

Not far from the Home Tree, nestled in the branches of a hawthorn, is Mother Dove, the most magical creature of all. She sits on her egg, watching over the fairies, who in turn watch over her. For as long as Mother Dove's egg stays well and whole, no one in Never Land will ever grow old.

Once, Mother Dove's egg *was* broken. But we are not telling the story of the egg here. Now it is time for Rosetta's tale. . . .

Rosetta's Dress Mess

"COMING THROUGH!" Rosetta called. "Watch your wings!" The pretty redhaired garden-talent fairy raced down a fourth-floor hallway of the Home Tree. Fairies and sparrow men dove aside as she rocketed past.

"Rosetta!" a fairy called out to her. "I love your shoes! Is that the new style?"

Rosetta sneaked an admiring look at her feet. They *were* darling shoes. It was so nice of Tally to notice!

"Yes!" Rosetta called back. "You should get a pair!" Then she raced on.

"Oh, Rosetta, wait up!" another fairy called to her. Rosetta slowed slightly. "Do these sleeves look better puffed out?" Melina asked. "Or pulled down?" She modeled the two options.

Rosetta took a moment to consider. "Puffed out," she decided. "But with that gorgeous hat, no one will be looking at your sleeves."

Melina beamed. A compliment from the best-dressed fairy in Pixie Hollow was enough to make any fairy's day!

Rosetta sped around a corner and

down another hallway. A sparrow man tried to ask her about his socks, but she waved him off. At the very end of the hall, she landed, at last, in front of a door. Above it hung a sign of cross-stitched letters on a framed square of fabric.

Rosetta's fairy glow flared with excitement as she rang the doorbell. Hem, a sewing-talent fairy, had made an announcement at breakfast in the tearoom. The sewing talents' next fashion show was going to take place in two days, just after sunset. Rosetta was determined to get a front-row seat.

You see, even though Rosetta was a garden-talent fairy, she loved pretty dresses . . . and shoes . . . and hats . . . and . . . Oh, peony petals! Rosetta loved clothes almost as much as she loved flowers!

At the last few shows, she had even gone backstage afterward for a closer look at the dresses. She had asked in her sweetest voice to try them on, and that had been that. It was hard for the sewing talents to get them back!

Hem opened the workshop door. "Rosetta!" she cried. "You look fantastic!" Rosetta struck a pose so Hem could see the dress better. "That African-violet dress. Those ribbon-grass slippers. Both are from our last show, I think!"

Rosetta smoothed a wrinkle out of the dress. When she replied, she tried to sound casual. "Oh, these?" she said. "I just threw them on this morning."

Hem grinned. Rosetta wasn't fooling anyone.

"Come in," Hem said. "You're not the only garden talent in the workshop today." She opened the door wider. Lily stood by one of the tables.

"I lost a button," Lily said. A sewing talent named Serena was stitching a new one onto Lily's tunic.

Rosetta gave Lily a quick wave, then turned back to Hem. "So, Hem, I was just . . ." Rosetta's voice trailed off. What *was* that sparkly cloth in the corner? Her eyes darted around the room. Bolts of spider silk, linen, Queen Anne's lace, and thistledown lined one wall. Bins brimmed with flowers, sorted by color and size. Baskets of dandelion fluff, acorn shells, and spools of thread in rainbow-color order filled shelves.

A dozen tables were set up around the workshop. By each table stood a fairy figure made from straw. The sewing talents fitted their designs on these forms. The straw forms came in all sizes—from that of the smallest fairy in Pixie Hollow to the tallest. That way, the sewing talents could make each outfit perfect.

Rosetta sighed, taking it all in. This was one of her favorite places in the Home Tree.

"Rosetta?" Hem said. "You were saying?"

"Oh!" Rosetta snapped out of it. "I was saying that I'm *so* excited about the fashion show!"

Hem smiled. "We are, too!"

"And I was just wondering." Rosetta clasped Hem's hand. "Could I take a teensy-weensy peek at the new dresses?"

Hem hesitated. "Well, but, I . . ."

Rosetta batted her long eyelashes. "Don't say no. I won't be able to wait *two whole days* to see them at the show!"

"Oh, all right," Hem said at last. "But don't go telling every fairy what they look like. The surprise is part of the fun!"

Rosetta promised. Then she was off, flying around the workshop.

She stopped in front of a lacy fern dress. Tack was sewing on tiny green sea-glass beads. "What beautiful beads!" Rosetta cried. Tack's fairy glow flared with pride.

Then Rosetta noticed a small pile of

clear beads on the table. "Wouldn't these clear ones reflect more light? They'd really make your dress sparkle."

Tack glared at Rosetta. "I like the green," he said.

Moving on to Taylor's worktable, Rosetta gasped. She ran her hand across the crinkly full skirt of Taylor's cornhusk dress. "How many layers does this have?"

"Four so far," Taylor said proudly. "Two more to go!"

"Looks fun to twirl in!" Rosetta said. "But . . ."

Taylor's brow wrinkled. "But what?" she asked.

"Well," Rosetta went on, "*I'd* add crinkly sleeves to match the crinkly skirt!"

Taylor crossed her arms and gave a soft *harrumph*.

Across the room, Lily overheard Rosetta's words and bit her lip. "I think Rosetta means," Lily piped up, "that the crinkliness is so beautiful . . . uh . . . she can't get enough of it! Right, Rosetta?"

But Rosetta didn't hear. She was already flying off toward the next table. *Designing dresses is fun!* Rosetta thought. *I'm really good at this!*

Serena, now done with Lily's button, was pinning a sash onto her design.

"That is such a pretty bathrobe!" Rosetta told her. "But where is your dress for the show?"

Serena ripped the sash off the dress. She crumpled it up and tossed it over her shoulder. "This *is* my dress for the show!" she said through gritted teeth.

Rosetta's fairy glow blushed. "Oh!" she said. "Silly me." She paused, trying to come up with a compliment. "It looks comfortable!" Then she hurried away.

Rosetta stopped to study every dress. She had a suggestion for each one. Niko, a sparrow man, was hemming a gardenia gown. "Poufier!" Rosetta cried. She held her hands out wide.

"Needs more bows!" she told another fairy. "It's all about bows!"

"Wider sleeves, finer lace, brighter color, and way more flowers!" she ordered someone else. Then she sweetly added, "Otherwise, it's perfect!"

Soon Rosetta had seen all the dresses.

She looked around the room. Her eyes twinkled. Her cheeks were flushed. On her face was a huge smile.

But none of the sewing talents smiled back. Not one. In fact, they all looked . . . annoyed.

"What?" Rosetta said. She turned to Hem. "What's the matter?"

Hem gently steered Rosetta toward the door. Lily followed. "It's nothing," Hem said. "We've just got a lot to do before the show!"

"Oh," said Rosetta. "Okay. But this was fun! Can I come back tomorrow?"

Every sewing talent turned to glare at Hem. What would she say?

Hem thought for a moment. "I have a better idea," she said. "You have a lot of opinions. Very strong opinions!" Several sewing talents looked at each other and nodded. "How would you like to design your *own* dress for the fashion show?"

Rosetta froze. Slowly, her eyes widened. She clasped her hands tightly. Her wings started to beat a mile a minute. But she didn't make a sound, until—

"*Eeeeeeeeeeeeeeee!*" Rosetta squealed loudly. Lily covered her ears.

When Rosetta took a breath, Lily rushed over and grabbed her hand. She pulled Rosetta away, out the door, and down the hall.

Over her shoulder, Lily called back to Hem. "I'm pretty sure that was a yes!"

Rosetta's head was still spinning as she and Lily flew outside into the Home Tree courtyard.

"Oh, my . . . I can't believe . . . a dress . . . my own design . . . wh-what will I make?" she stammered. "Two days! That's not a lot of time."

"Not a lot of time for what?" came a

voice nearby. Silvermist, a water-talent fairy, peeked out from under an umbrella plant. She was collecting dewdrops in a shiny shell pitcher.

"Oh, Silvermist!" Rosetta cried. She landed near her friend. "Listen to this. The sewing talents asked me to design a dress for the fashion show! Can you believe it?" She giggled.

"Babbling brooks!" cried Silvermist. "That's fantastic, Rosetta!"

"I know," Rosetta went on. "I was giving them advice on their latest dresses. I guess they really loved my ideas."

Next to Rosetta, Lily cleared her throat. "Uh," she said. "That's not *exactly* how it went."

Rosetta frowned. "What do you

mean?" she cried. Then her face brightened. "Oh! You're right. I left out the part where Hem said I'm a very strong designer."

Lily put a hand on Rosetta's shoulder. "No, Rosetta," she said gently, "Hem said you have very strong *opinions*. And I'm not sure she meant it in a good way." Lily looked pained to remember it. "I think you might have hurt their feelings."

"Hurt their feelings?" Rosetta repeated, shocked. "I just pointed out ways their dresses could be better." She shrugged. "That's helpful, not hurtful."

Lily nodded. "But how would you feel if a sewing talent came and suggested ways to make your garden prettier? Designing is like that for the sewing talents."

Rosetta gave a half-snort. "Lily, that's different. *I* have a knack for designing dresses." *Really,* she thought. *A sewing talent who could improve on my garden? I'd like to see that!*

"I think Lily's right," Silvermist said. She lifted a dewdrop off a leaf. It sat, round and unbroken, in the palm of her hand. "If you told me you had a better way to gather dewdrops, I'd get teary-eyed."

Rosetta was about to point out that water fairies got teary at just about everything. But at that moment, Fira, a light talent, flew up in a tizzy.

"Rosetta!" Fira cried. "You have to

help me. All the light talents are having lunch with Queen Clarion tomorrow. And I have no idea what to wear!"

Rosetta's glow turned pink. "I'd be happy to help!" Then, with a flip of her flowing red hair and a quick wave to Lily and Silvermist, she zipped away with Fira.

Lily's a sweet pea, Rosetta thought as she flew. *But sometimes she's a little too sensitive. Hurt feelings?* Rosetta didn't think so. Maybe the sewing talents were . . . jealous? What if it turned out a garden fairy could design a better dress?

Later, back in her room, Rosetta was ready to work on her dress design. She threw open the doors of her wardrobe.

Rosetta bet she had more dresses than any other fairy in Pixie Hollow. She had so many, in fact, that they didn't all fit in one regular wardrobe. She had asked Tinker Bell to make her a special one. It had wheels and spun around. On the back side was another pair of doors—and a second clothing compartment. But even with double the storage, Rosetta's wardrobe was packed full.

Rosetta looked through her dresses. She loved every single one of them. But she wanted to make something totally new.

She grabbed a leaf-scroll and a feather pen from her writing desk. She jotted down a few quick notes. Then, scroll and pen in hand, she darted out of her room.

First I need to pick the color, she thought. And where better to start than in one of the most colorful spots in Pixie Hollow? Her own garden!

When she got there, she flew past the roses. They were her favorite flower, but she had tons of rose dresses. The same was true for daffodils, irises, tulips, daisies, lilies, honeysuckle, and pansies. Rosetta flitted all around the garden. Nope. Her dress material just wasn't here.

If not flower petals, then . . . leaves? Spider silk? Thistledown? No. It couldn't be anything that was on a shelf in the sewing workshop.

Rosetta heard rustling from the other side of some azaleas. She put her hands on her hips. That had better not be squirrels, digging up her baby bulbs again! She poked her head through the branches, ready to scold. Instead, she gasped. Two hummingbirds were darting from flower to flower, sipping nectar.

As far as animals went, Rosetta didn't have a favorite. They were all either too dirty, too skittish, too loud, or too . . . wild. But even Rosetta liked hummingbirds. They carried pollen from

flower to flower, helping to make new ones. Best of all, they had the most beautiful feathers.

Rosetta tapped her feather pen on her scroll. Then, staring at the pen as if for the first time, she cried out.

"Feathers!" She quickly wrote it down. Now, *there* was an unusual choice for a dress. "*Hummingbird* feathers! That's it!"

Rosetta had never, *ever* seen a dress made from shimmering hummingbird feathers. No wonder! Feathers of any kind were hard to come by. It would take forever to gather enough fallen feathers. It would be better to find a bird willing to give up some of his own.

But hummingbirds were so fast. And

so fidgety! It wore her out just thinking about their constant darting this way and that.

Luckily, Rosetta knew a certain animal talent who had a good hummingbird friend named Twitter. "I need to talk to Beck!" she cried.

Rosetta looked down at her leaf-scroll. A hummingbird-feather dress! With a purple thistle-puff hat? And some lady-slipper slippers!

Her design would knock the sewing talents' socks off!

3

Rosetta headed straight for Beck's room. Near the Home Tree, she heard banging from the side of the old maple. Curious, she veered off course to check it out. She followed the curve of the great trunk around to the courtyard.

It was buzzing with activity. Dozens of fairies and sparrow men were hard at work. Woodworking fairies nailed twigs together, making a walkway. Posts raised it off the ground to about the height of a fairy. Painting fairies brushed on a coat of yellow mustard-seed paint.

Then Rosetta noticed Hem and some other sewing talents in the walkway's shadow. They held birch-bark clipboards and shouted out instructions.

Rosetta rushed over. "Hem! Is this—?"

"The runway for the fashion show!" Hem told her. Then she called to the carpenters, "More floorboards over here!"

Rosetta gave a tiny squeal of excitement. She could picture it now. Every fairy's eyes on her dress. She'd fly over the runway, into the center of the courtyard. The shimmery feathers would catch the light of the firefly lanterns.

Rosetta studied the runway from every angle. How would her dress look to each fairy in the audience?

"Oh, Hem!" Rosetta called across the courtyard. "The runway needs to be longer. Fairies over here won't be able to see me—I mean, us." Rosetta flew over to Hem, who stood on the unfinished runway. But Hem didn't look up from her clipboard.

Rosetta cleared her throat. "And don't you think there should be twice as many firefly lanterns?"

Hem waved the woodworking fairies over. They each carried a floorboard.

"Hem?" Rosetta moved in closer. "What do you think about a darker paint on the runway? A deep red would

contrast with my dress so nicely. Hem? Hem?" She snapped her fingers in Hem's face.

Hem sighed. "Rosetta, please—"

Sandy, one of the woodworking fairies, turned around suddenly. She didn't know Rosetta had moved close behind her. *Thwap!* The floorboard on Sandy's shoulder whacked Rosetta right on the back of her head!

Flump! Rosetta dropped like a sack of acorns at the end of the runway.

"Knotty pines! Is she okay?" cried Sandy.

"Rosetta!" Hem gasped, kneeling at her side. "Rosetta? Can you hear me?"

Everyone breathed a sigh of relief when Rosetta opened her eyes. Hem, Sandy, and lots of sewing and woodworking talents stood over her.

"Oh, Rosetta!" Sandy moaned. "I'd fly backward if I could!

"Are you okay?" Hem asked.

Rosetta rubbed the back of her head. "What happened?" she asked. She sat up slowly.

"Take it easy," Hem said. "You were knocked out for a few wingbeats." She explained about Sandy and the floorboard.

Rosetta stayed put for several minutes. Her ears were ringing and her head did feel a bit fuzzy. But slowly, it cleared. It was all coming back to her.

She remembered the fashion show and the hummingbird-feather dress. She had been going to see Beck.

Rosetta tried standing. She brushed some sawdust from her hair. When her knees stopped shaking, she rose into the air. With each minute, her wings felt stronger and her head felt less foggy. "I'm fine, really," she told Hem and Sandy.

"Are you sure?" Hem asked. "Maybe we should take you to the nursing talents? Just to be safe."

But Rosetta waved Hem's concern away. As she flew off toward Beck's room, she called back over her shoulder. "I've got to go! I've got a dress to make!" Rosetta couldn't help adding, "It's going to be a showstopper!"

She was still rubbing her head as she landed in front of Beck's door. *That was a good whack,* she thought. *But it'll take more than that to stop me!*

She knocked and heard Beck call, "Come in!"

She opened the door to find Beck knee-deep in chestnuts. She was stacking them neatly in baskets. They were treats for her squirrel friends.

"Beck, I need your help!" Rosetta blurted out. She quickly described her dress idea for the fashion show and her need for feathers. Then she stopped in the middle of a sentence.

"Your hair looks great, by the way," she told Beck. "Have you done something different?"

Beck stared at Rosetta. The stare became a squint. "Are you teasing me?" Beck asked. She tried to smooth her tangled hair. "I've been gathering chestnuts in the underbrush all day."

"No, I'm serious," said Rosetta.

Beck eyed her, waiting for the punch line. When it didn't come, she shrugged. "It's just you never like my hair." She looked down at her simple leaf dress. She had ten of them—all the same. "Or my clothes."

Huh, thought Rosetta. Now that she looked more closely, Beck's hair did look mostly . . . messy. She rubbed her head. It still felt a little fuzzy.

"So anyway," Rosetta said, getting back to her question, "could you ask

Twitter if he could spare some feathers?"

Beck shook her head. "I can't do that. Twitter just molted. So did the other hummingbirds."

Rosetta scrunched up her nose. "Eeww," she said. "That sounds icky." She definitely did not want any moldy feathers in her dress. "But . . . maybe

I could just scrape all the mold off?"

Beck laughed out loud, knocking a chestnut off the pile. "Not 'molded,'" she said. "*Molted*. That's when birds lose a lot of their feathers. Over time, new ones grow in."

"Oh!" said Rosetta. "Where are all the feathers they lost?"

Beck shrugged. "Who knows?" she replied as she started stacking chestnuts again. "Some here. Some there. Most get carried off by the wind, I guess."

Rosetta groaned. What a waste! All those gorgeous feathers. Dresses and dresses' worth of feathers, gone!

Then she had a brilliant idea. "I'll just take some of their new feathers!" she suggested. "I bet the new ones are more shimmery than the old ones!"

Beck stopped stacking and turned to face Rosetta. "You don't understand, Rosetta. The new ones take weeks to grow in fully. And plucking feathers hurts the birds."

Rosetta felt as if someone had just yanked her roots out of the ground. *Of all the times for birds to choose to molt!* she thought. *Right before a fashion show!*

No shimmery feathers. No dress.

What would she do now?

4

ROSETTA WAS BACK to square one. She had to think of another unique, show-stopping dress design. But she wasn't worried. After all, she was the best-dressed fairy in Pixie Hollow. She was sure she'd come up with lots of good ideas. She would crisscross Pixie Hollow if she had to.

Her garden didn't have anything she

wanted to use. But maybe someone else's did. Like Lily's!

Lily gave Rosetta a tour, pointing out her most unusual flowers—orchids, lotuses, and a rare type of daisy with rainbow petals. But nothing jumped out at Rosetta. Nothing was nearly as dazzling as shimmering hummingbird feathers.

"Maybe some strawberry blooms?" Lily asked. "They're very sweet."

Rosetta looked around Lily's tidy garden. Suddenly, a thought struck like a snapdragon snap. She was so caught up in the fashion show, she hadn't done a single thing in her own garden!

"Oh, sunflower seeds!" she exclaimed. "I haven't watered. I haven't weeded. What kind of garden fairy am I?"

Lily patted Rosetta's hand. "I knew you'd come arou—"

Rosetta cut her off. "I'm so glad you understand!" She flashed her biggest, sweetest smile. "So you'll keep an eye on my garden for me? Just until after the fashion show?"

Lily raised one eyebrow. "Me? Uh, sure, Rosetta. I'd be happy to."

Rosetta smiled. That was a relief. Dress or no dress, she knew her garden was in excellent hands.

Rosetta thought about trying another garden. Aster's. Or Bluebell's. But she decided to go somewhere else instead. She left Lily's garden and stopped in at Bess's art studio. She told Bess that she was making a dress for the fashion show. "I figure art fairies know about color and design," Rosetta said. "Maybe I'll be inspired by one of your paintings!"

Rosetta loved Bess's landscapes of Pixie Hollow. She loved her portraits of Queen Clarion and all of Bess's friends. Rosetta especially loved a painting Bess had done of her. "The white-rose dress really sets off the blue of my eyes," Rosetta pointed out.

But she didn't get an idea for her design. As she turned to go, something on a hook by the door caught her eye.

She lifted the thin cotton garment off the hook. It had the most unusual pattern, with splotches of color here and there. "How interesting! Bess, which sewing-talent fairy made this?"

Bess gave her an odd look. "Which sewing talent?" Bess repeated. "Umm . . . that's an art smock."

Rosetta's glow went pink. Flustered, she tried to cover up her mistake. "Oh, uh . . . of course! I knew that." Still . . . she wanted to try something. "Can I see it on you?"

Bess put the smock over her tunic and leggings. Rosetta grabbed a length of picture-hanging cord from a table. She tied the cord around Bess's waist like a belt. Then she steered Bess over to a mirror.

"Well?" Rosetta said. She hovered behind Bess as they both looked at her reflection. "What do you think?"

Bess hesitated. "I think . . ." She

seemed to be searching for the right words. "I think it looks like an art smock. With a picture-hanging cord for a belt."

Rosetta's shoulders drooped like a daisy in need of water. *She's right*, Rosetta thought. *I'm so desperate for a great idea, I'm letting it get to me!*

Rosetta's visit to Silvermist's room was no help, either. The water-talent fairy had beautiful bowls and pitchers made from shiny shells and mother-of-pearl. Bits of colored sea glass decorated her dressing table. Smooth river rocks framed her mirror. But strangely, Rosetta was drawn to the thimble holding beach pebbles in the corner.

"Would this make a good hat?" she asked Silvermist.

Silvermist thought it over. "If you're a construction fairy, maybe?" she replied.

By dinnertime, Rosetta felt completely lost. Designing a dress was harder than it looked. She only had tomorrow and part of the next day! And she wasn't very fast at sewing! If she didn't think of something soon, she wouldn't have time to make *any* dress.

She considered the tablecloths and the heavy drapes in the tearoom. *I could sew together floral-print cloth napkins,* she thought. *You wouldn't have to worry about spilling on it.* She shook her head, scrapping the idea.

She studied a winterberry branch in the table's centerpiece. *Berries are beautiful,* she thought. Could she string them into a dress? Then she imagined what it would feel like to sit down. *Squish!*

Rosetta anxiously tapped her fingers on the table. There had to be an idea here!

At that moment, a fairy floated past her. Wait! What was she wearing? The fairy's garment was simple, even plain, in a stiff, heavy fabric, with some kind of small bow in the back.

It was a full minute before Rosetta realized what she was looking at. The fairy was Dulcie, a baking talent. And she was wearing an apron.

A plain kitchen apron.

Rosetta could not leave the tearoom quickly enough. "I'm not feeling so hungry after all," she told Lily, who was sitting next to her. Then she bolted out as fast as her wings could carry her.

"What is wrong with me?" Rosetta wondered aloud as she made a beeline for her room. All she wanted was to sit quietly and think. First Bess's art smock, then Silvermist's bucket. And now Dulcie's apron? A napkin dress? A berry dress? Rosetta had been making style missteps all day. And then there had been that moment at Beck's. Her messed-up hair had seemed pretty.

Rosetta hadn't had one good fashion idea since morning.

She gasped and stopped in midair. "Before I got hit on the head!" she cried. Before that, the good ideas—the feather dress, the thistle-puff hat, the slippers— had been coming fast and furious. Since then, nothing! It was as if the knock on the head had changed her.

It was as if . . . she had *lost* her sense of style!

5

THAT NIGHT, ROSETTA slept terribly. She had a bad dream. In it, she was going to Queen Clarion's party. She was dressed up in a hummingbird-feather dress, a purple thistle-puff hat, and lady-slipper slippers. She walked confidently into the courtyard. Heads turned. All eyes were on her. She smiled. But no one smiled back. They were all staring at her dress. Rosetta looked down. The feathers were gone. In their place were dozens of Dulcie's famous poppy puff rolls.

Rosetta woke in a panic. Outside the window, the light gray sky told her it was still very early in the morning. It had just been a dream.

She lay back down and put her pillow over her face. A poppy puff dress? Was that what she had come to? But . . . was it such a terrible idea? Maybe with a little sugar frosting for color?

No! She threw the pillow across the room. It knocked the lampshade off her firefly lamp. What was she thinking? Even without any style sense, she knew that a poppy-puff-roll dress was a bad idea.

She pushed off her thistledown blanket and got up. "Today is a new day," she said. "Maybe I'm back to my old self."

But one look inside her wardrobe and her fears flooded back. It was packed with beautiful clothes. And she had no idea what to wear.

Rosetta's heart sank. The fashion show was the next day. She didn't have a dress. She didn't have a plan. And now she didn't really have a hope. If anything, she was more confused than yesterday. This morning, she couldn't even pick out something to wear! Was it all because of the bump on the head?

Rosetta reached into her wardrobe. She grabbed a skirt and top and threw them on. Then she scooped a sun hat up off the floor. Even a fairy with no sense of style knows to protect her face from the sun. The last thing she needed was a sunburn.

A few minutes later, a mopey Rosetta flew slowly into the tearoom. It was still early for breakfast. Only a few other fairies were scattered around the room—mostly baking and serving talents. Then Rosetta noticed Tinker Bell at the pots-and-pans-talent table. Tink waved Rosetta over.

"Wow!" Tink cried. "That's some outfit!"

"Is it?" Rosetta asked, hope filling her voice. Maybe she had come up with a brilliant outfit without even trying! She looked down at her clothes. She was wearing a two-toned ivy skirt. An eye-catching patch of bright yellow blazed in the center of each green leaf. She had paired the skirt with a puffy-sleeved blouse of cardinal flower and hot-pink anemone petals. The mix of colors was dizzying!

Tink pointed to the hat on Rosetta's head. "Is that . . . a lampshade?"

Rosetta took it off and looked at it for the first time. "I guess it is," she said. Maybe that was why the baking fairies kept looking over at her. She shrugged and put it back on her head. She was too worried to care. So what if other fairies laughed at her?

"What are you doing up so early?" she asked Tink.

"Just hungry," Tink replied. "How about you?"

"I woke up and couldn't get back to sleep." Rosetta felt tears welling in her eyes. "Because my fashion sense got knocked out of me yesterday. I've probably lost it forever." She dropped into the chair next to Tink. Putting her head down on the table, she let the tears spill out. In between sobs, she tried to explain.

Tink tugged her bangs and frowned. She was having trouble understanding Rosetta's high-pitched sob-speak. At last, her face brightened.

"Fashion sense?" she said. "Who needs it? Now you probably have more *common* sense! Just look at me. I wear the same thing every day."

Rosetta did look at Tink. Then she put down her head again and wailed. The same thing? Every day? How tragic!

Tink looked around. The serving talents were starting to stare. "Shhh, Rosetta," she hushed. "Quiet down. That's enough. Oh, all right, I'll help you, I'll help you! Just stop crying already."

"Tink, are you sure this is a good idea?" Rosetta asked.

"Have you got a better one?" Tink replied.

"No," said Rosetta.

"Then let's give it a try!" Tink said. "It could work!"

Rosetta still wasn't sure. They were

standing on the fashion show runway. It was still early in the morning. Not another fairy was in sight.

Tink's idea was simple. "A whack on the head knocked your fashion sense out of whack. So maybe another will whack it back into place!" she explained for the fifth time. Rosetta shivered. She didn't like the gleam in Tink's eye whenever she said the word "whack."

They had found some extra floorboards under the runway. Tink took a few practice swings with one.

Leave it to Tink to try to fix me the same way she fixes her pots and pans! Rosetta thought.

"Hold still," Tink told her. "On the count of three—"

"Wait!" Rosetta cried. "I'm not ready yet." This was crazy, but the truth was, she really, *really* wanted to design a dress for the show. The clock was ticking.

"Let's go," Rosetta said at last. "What's the worst that could happen?" Tink opened her mouth to reply. But Rosetta quickly added, "Don't answer that." She took a deep breath. "Not too hard," she said firmly. "And try not to mess up my hair." Then she turned her back on Tink. She closed her eyes and braced for the blow.

Tink wound up and—

Rosetta ducked. The board sailed over her head and Tink spun around in a full circle.

"No, don't!" Rosetta covered her head

with her hand. She stayed like that for several long moments. Then she stood up straight and tall again. She closed her eyes. "Okay. I'm ready now."

"Are you sure?" Tink waited until Rosetta nodded. "Here goes. One . . . two . . . th—"

"*AAAH!*" Rosetta ducked again. "I can't help it! I just—it's really hard to—"

"Let someone hit you with a board?" Tink said. She looked at the inch-long piece of wood in her hands. "I can't say that I blame you."

"Oooooo!" Rosetta stomped her dainty slippered foot. "But how can I let this idea go without even trying it? I'll never know if it would have worked!"

Tink lowered the floorboard. The two fairies sat down side by side on the runway.

Tink rested her hand on her chin and tugged on her bangs. Rosetta crossed her ankles and curled a strand of hair around her finger. Both were deep in thought.

Then Tink sat bolt upright. "Aha!" she said. "What if you don't *know* when

I'm going to whack you on the head?"

"What?" said Rosetta.

"I could follow you around," Tink said, her eyes lighting up. "In secret!"

"You mean you'd sneak up on me?" Rosetta said. Her brow wrinkled prettily. "That way, I can't duck or avoid it?"

Tink nodded.

"You'd do that?" Rosetta said. She smiled sweetly at Tink. "For me?"

Tinker Bell shrugged. "What are friends for?"

6

ROSETTA AND TINK agreed on three rules. First, Tink couldn't hit Rosetta too hard. Second, no sneaking up on her while she was sleeping. And third, Tink wasn't allowed to tell anyone about it.

"After all, I don't want everyone to know I've lost my style!" Rosetta said.

Rosetta and Tink shook hands on it. Then they flew off in different directions.

Rosetta headed for her garden. She had two goals for the day. Make a dress. And keep busy, keep busy, keep busy. If she sat around waiting for Tink to strike, she'd go crazy.

Rosetta had to admit, spending time with Tink had changed her attitude. Tink was a real go-getter. She'd never just sit around crying about a problem. No, Tink would do something about it. An hour ago, Rosetta had been ready to give up. But it wasn't too late. She could still make a dress to impress all the fairies.

"I'm going to find lots of pretty things," she vowed. "I'm going to bring them back. And I'm going to make them into a dress!" Her shoulders drooped slightly. "Somehow," she whispered.

As Rosetta neared her garden, her spirits lifted. She hadn't been there for a day, and she missed it. She missed the sun on the daylilies and the dew-speckled violets. She missed the colors, smells, and sounds of her garden.

Rosetta flew through the climbing-rose arch that was the garden's grandest entrance. She took a deep breath. Right away, her problems seemed smaller.

She looked around. She thought she'd find weeds popping up. But she didn't. She also didn't see a single wilting primrose or bent sunflower stalk in need of staking. Her garden looked as if she hadn't been gone at all.

She suddenly realized why. "Lily!" she cried.

"Yes?" said a voice to her right. Up popped Lily's head from behind a patch of buttercups.

"Oh!" cried Rosetta, startled. "Lily, you're here! The garden looks so lovely. You're so sweet to take care of it for me!"

"Rosetta! It's you!" said Lily. "I didn't recognize you at first in that . . . really interesting hat."

Rosetta put a hand to her head. *Oops!* She'd forgotten to take off the lampshade. Oh well, it *was* doing an outstanding job of shading her nose.

Another familiar face popped up next to Lily's.

"Silvermist!" Rosetta cried.

The water-talent fairy gave Rosetta a little wave. She held up a walnut-shell bucket. "I'm just helping out with the watering."

"That's so nice of you!" Rosetta said. She knew she should feel grateful. Lily and Silvermist were doing her a huge favor. But she felt a pang of jealousy, too. *Nearly a full day without me,* thought Rosetta. *And my flowers seem as happy as ever. Happier, even. It's as if they don't need me at all!*

"Are you done with the dress?" Silvermist asked. "I can't wait to see it."

Her question shook Rosetta back to her plan for the day. "Actually, I was about to head out," she said. She crossed her fingers behind her back. "To look for finishing touches." *It's not a complete fib,* she added in her head.

Lily's eyes went wide, and Silvermist's wings beat faster. "I'd love to come with you!" Silvermist exclaimed.

"Oh, yes!" said Lily. "Can we, Rosetta? It would be a treat to watch a genius at work!"

Rosetta hesitated. "Uh, a genius . . . You don't have to do that." She didn't have a clue what she was looking for! It would be very obvious. "You've both been so helpful already."

"But it would be fun!" Lily insisted.

"And you can't possibly carry everything back by yourself," Silvermist said.

Rosetta tried to talk them out of it. But in the end, she just couldn't say no.

With Lily and Silvermist following, Rosetta led the way. *Where to?* she wondered. The first thing that popped into her head was Havendish Stream. So she flew in that direction.

"So what are you looking for?" Lily asked.

"Oh, you know," Rosetta said. She tried to sound relaxed. "A little of this. A little of that."

Silvermist chuckled. "I get it. You don't want to give anything away. Your design is top-secret. Hmm?"

If only! Rosetta thought. But if they thought she was being mysterious . . . Well, maybe that could work.

Rosetta hovered and looked around Havendish Stream. Lily and Silvermist stopped and watched her. She felt their eyes on her.

She had to choose something here. But what? Directly below her was a moss-covered rock. "Aha!" she exclaimed, as if she had been looking for it all along. She tore off a large piece of the soft green plant. She rolled it up and tucked it under one arm.

Lily and Silvermist nodded. "Moss," said Lily. "Interesting."

They watched Rosetta fly haltingly this way and that. She wandered toward some reeds at the water's edge. She pulled three of them. Then she plucked a small heart-shaped lily pad from the stream. She handed the items to Silvermist. "Could you carry these?" she asked.

"Of course!" Silvermist replied. She looked at the hodgepodge of things in her hands. Jokingly, she suggested another item. "How about those waterlogged bits of woodrush over there?"

"Oh, uh, yes! That might work, too," Rosetta replied. *I can't imagine how,* she thought. *But I might be missing something. Maybe bringing Silvermist and Lily along was a good idea after all!*

At Rosetta's reply, Silvermist's merry expression clouded with confusion. She and Lily followed Rosetta away from the stream. They flew deeper into the woods. On the way, Rosetta picked up some drab toadstools.

Silvermist winked at Lily and pointed to a piece of pine branch. "How about this?" she asked Rosetta.

"Um . . . sure!" Rosetta said.

"And this?" Silvermist tried. She held up a strange-looking seedpod.

Rosetta hesitated and looked it over. "Yes, let's take that." She couldn't think of a good reason not to.

Silvermist handed some of the items to Lily for her to carry. "So, you . . . have plans for these things, Rosetta?"

"What?" Rosetta said. "Uh, yes." But she didn't sound very sure of herself.

Flying through the dairy mouse pasture, Rosetta picked five cloverleaf stems. She left the pink clover flowers behind.

"Don't you want the flowers?" Lily asked her. "They're pretty." Then, with a glance at the browns and greens of their armloads, she added, "And colorful."

"Oh! Of course," said Rosetta, trying to cover. How could she, a garden talent, have overlooked the flowers!

Silvermist was eyeing Rosetta. As they headed back into the woods, Silvermist flew close beside her.

"Rosetta, are you feeling okay?" she asked. "You don't seem yourself."

Rosetta forced a laugh. "Wh-what do

you mean?" she said. She stopped by the trunk of a large oak. Lily and Silvermist stopped, too. "I'm fine. Just fine." Rosetta felt a pang of guilt. Silvermist and Lily were being good friends to her, and she was fibbing to them.

Silvermist's eyes narrowed. "Really?" she asked. "If I didn't know better, I'd guess you have no idea what you're looking for."

Rosetta stared up at the sky, down at the ground—anywhere but at Silvermist. She opened her mouth to answer. She wasn't sure what words would come out.

Just then, in a flash, a blond-haired fairy in a short green leaf-dress zipped out from behind the oak tree. She swung a large stick at Rosetta's head.

"Rosetta, duck!" Silvermist yelled. The stick whistled over Rosetta's head, missing it by a hair.

"Tinker Bell!" Lily gasped. "What in Pixie Hollow are you doing?"

7

Rosetta held up her hands to calm Silvermist and Lily. "It's okay! Tink's trying to help me."

"Help you?" Lily said. "She just tried to bonk you on the head with a stick!"

Rosetta took a deep breath. "I know. It doesn't make sense. But it's the truth."

Rosetta told them the whole story.

She started with her hummingbird-feather dress idea. She told them about the knock on the head at the runway.

"Right before that, I had designed an amazingly fantastic outfit! And right after, I complimented *Beck* on her *hair*!"

"Ooooh," said Silvermist. Her face was grim. "That doesn't sound like you."

Rosetta went on. She described her frustration ever since the blow to her head. And she told them about her talk with Tink and their plan to knock some fashion sense back into her.

Silvermist and Lily were quiet for a moment. They let Rosetta's story sink in. Then Silvermist said, "Well, I guess that would explain your outfit, Rosetta." She turned to Tink. "But Tink, really?

Sneaking around? Trying to knock your friend on the head?"

"It could work!" Tink insisted.

"And I want to give it a try," Rosetta added. "Something definitely happened when that floorboard hit me." She plopped down on a mound of dry pine needles. Her shoulders slumped. "I just want to feel like my old self again."

Silvermist, Lily, and Tink flew to Rosetta's side. Silvermist wrapped an arm around her shoulder. "Aw, cheer up, Rosetta," Silvermist said. "We are, after all, just talking about *clothes*—"

"But I—" Rosetta interrupted.

"And I *know*," Silvermist went on, "clothes are something you like a lot. So Rosetta, I'd like to introduce you to some fairies who can help you."

"Who?" asked Rosetta.

Silvermist flew between Tink and Lily. She put an arm around each of them. "Us!" she exclaimed.

Lily's face lit up. "Yes!" she said. "We'll help you make a dress."

Rosetta thought about it. Yesterday she would have said no. She had felt confident she knew best. She had wanted the design to be hers—all hers.

But a lot had changed since then. And Rosetta felt better now that her friends were around her.

She smiled a big smile. "Would you do that? Really?"

"Of course!" Lily cried.

"Absolutely!" Silvermist agreed.

But Tink's brow was wrinkled. She looked unsure.

"Clothes? They're not my thing," she said. Then an idea seemed to come to her. "But I'm in *if* I can keep my old job, too."

"What?" said Lily. "Do you mean hitting Rosetta on the head when she's not looking?"

Tink nodded and grinned.

"Deal," Rosetta said. She still wanted to try out Tink's idea. In the meantime, with her friends' help, she could be making a dress. *Maybe this can all work out*, she thought. *By the fashion show tomorrow, Tink will have bonked me on the head. I'll be all better, and I'll have a dress!*

With the toe of her slipper, Tink kicked at the moss. "Do you want to take this . . . stuff?" she asked Rosetta.

Rosetta took one look at the pile of brown toadstools, seedpods, and pine needles. She shuddered. "Leave it," she said. "I don't know what I was thinking."

The four fairies headed back toward the Home Tree. When they reached the courtyard, Rosetta stopped. The others huddled up around her.

"Here's the plan," said Rosetta. "Let's split up. Grab a few things we might be able to use. Then meet back in my room. I'll get us some dinner from the kitchen." She realized she hadn't eaten since breakfast. She definitely couldn't be creative on an empty stomach!

They all zipped off in different directions. Rosetta headed for her room. In the lobby of the Home Tree, she passed a group of baking fairies. Three of them were wearing unusual hats.

Rosetta looked closer. Were they hats? Or . . .

Lampshades! Rosetta couldn't help giggling. *Well, that's something,* she thought. *I've lost my sense of style. But I'm still a trendsetter!*

8

"WHAT'S KEEPING Tinker Bell?" Rosetta wondered. Outside, the moon was up.

She fluttered around her room as Lily and Silvermist unpacked their finds. The three of them had finished their cups of pumpkin soup. But Tink's stood untasted, getting cold, on a side table.

A knock came at the door. "Oh, good! That must be her!" Rosetta flew across the room. She threw open the door. "Whoa!" she cried, darting backward.

Stick in hand, Tink had taken a quick swing at her.

"Nice try, Tink," said Rosetta. "But I knew it was you."

Tink snapped her fingers. "So close!" She picked up a wooden crate next to the door and took it into Rosetta's room.

The fairies gathered at the foot of Rosetta's bed. "Okay," she said. "What have we got?"

Silvermist went first. She showed them a seaweed bag filled with blue sea-glass beads and bits of shiny shells. "This is my favorite part," she said, pulling out a deep-purple water lily blossom. "The dress could be long and flowing, with seaglass and shells for sparkle!"

Rosetta nodded. "Very pretty," she said. "Very . . . water fairy."

Silvermist laughed, then shrugged. "That's me!"

Lily went next. She held up an orange tiger lily blossom and several handfuls of pink phlox buds. She also had one perfectly shaped red tulip. "How about a tulip skirt, a phlox-bud top, and a tiger lily hat?"

Silvermist's eyes grew wide. "All those colors? In the same outfit?"

Rosetta liked bright colors. But would it be too much? She didn't trust herself to know anymore.

"You're going to love what I brought," Tink said. She upended her crate with a loud *clatter, clatter, clunk*. Several pieces of copper lay in a heap with a hammer and what looked like a teapot handle.

"Oh, wait!" Tink cried, picking up the hammer. "That's not for the dress. That's for me." She jammed it into the tool belt she was wearing. "This dress

needs some tinker touches. Something metallic. Definitely."

The other three stared at Tink's pile. They all looked skeptical.

"So, Rosetta," said Silvermist, "how about you?"

"I had some ideas about a hat and shoes," Rosetta said. She held up a spiky purple thistle puff and some lady-slipper flowers from her garden. "As for the dress, I'm stumped."

"That's okay," said Lily. "Silvermist, Tink, and I have plenty of ideas."

Silvermist nodded. "Which did you like best?"

Rosetta thought about it. "Well . . . I . . . hmm . . ."

"Long and flowing would be very

fancy," Silvermist pointed out. "Just right for the fashion show."

Lily turned her tulip upside down. She held it against her waist, modeling it as a skirt. "But a tulip dress would be playful," she said.

"No, no," said Tink. "We've all seen dresses like those. But have any of you *ever* seen a copper dress?"

Silvermist chortled. "No, and there's a good reason for that," she said.

Tink, Silvermist, and Lily turned back to Rosetta. She knew they were waiting for her decision. But she had no idea what to say.

Finally, she threw up her hands. "I don't know!" she cried. "Each of you has a different style. And at the moment,

I don't have any! How am I supposed to decide?" She flopped down onto her bed. "We can't use them all."

The room was silent for a moment. Then Rosetta suddenly sat up. "Wait! Maybe we *can* use them all!"

Lily sat next to Rosetta. "Really?" she said. "How?"

"What if we each make a part of the dress?" Rosetta explained. "Then we'll put the pieces together and . . . *ta-da!*"

Lily nodded. "That just *might* work."

Silvermist agreed. "It would be different, anyway."

Tink offered Rosetta and Lily each a hand. They grabbed on, and Tink pulled them up off the bed. "Sounds good to me!" she said.

Time was ticking away. So they agreed on a plan. Silvermist would make the skirt. Lily would make the top. Tink would handle the sleeves. And Rosetta would make the hat and slippers she had dreamed up earlier.

Each fairy picked a corner of Rosetta's room. They settled in and got right to work. For the better part of two hours, the room was quiet, except for random hammering from Tink's corner.

At one point, Rosetta noticed she hadn't heard Tink's hammering in a while. Then the quiet was broken by the whir of wings close behind her.

"I hear you, Tink," said Rosetta. She knew without looking up that Tink was trying to sneak up on her.

"So close!" Tink whispered. She dropped her stick and flew back to her corner.

Not long after that, the fairies gathered together once again. They took turns pinning their parts of the dress to a straw fairy form Rosetta kept next to her wardrobe.

Rosetta was the last. She placed the thistle-puff hat on the straw fairy's head. She set the lady-slipper slippers at its base. Then they all took a step back and studied the outfit.

Lily had pieced all three flowers— the red tulip, the orange lily, and the pink phlox—in an eye-catching top. Meanwhile, Silvermist's skirt was loaded with sea-glass and shells sewn in a swirl

pattern. For the sleeves, Tink had lashed together copper bangles. Each piece of the dress was beautiful in its way. But all together, with the spiky thistle-puff hat and the lavender lady-slipper slippers, the outfit was . . .

"It's definitely one of a kind!" Tink offered.

"Yes," Lily agreed. She tilted her head to one side and stared hard at the dress. "That is really something."

"Something . . . unusual," Silvermist said. At first, Rosetta was speechless. Then she realized she was having the strongest reaction she'd had in two days.

"Weeping willows!" she exclaimed. "That is *awful*."

9

THE NEXT MORNING, Rosetta rolled over in bed and opened her eyes. She had the feeling of something important left undone. *The fashion show,* she thought. *Today!*

Rosetta squinted at the crazy mess of a dress hanging on the door of her wardrobe. She laughed just looking at it. The night before, all four fairies had

had a good laugh, too—after the disappointment had worn off.

Rosetta sighed and got out of bed. They had given it a try, and that was that. Today at sunset, the sewing talents would put on the fashion show. But Rosetta wouldn't have a dress in it. What would the sewing fairies think? Her glow turned pink with embarrassment. She had been so haughty in the sewing room. She hated to even remember that day and all the things she had said.

Face it! thought Rosetta. *I'm not a sewing talent. I'm a garden-talent fairy.* She froze. The thought wasn't meant to be comforting, but it was, somehow. She ran it through her head again. "I'm a garden fairy!" she repeated out loud.

She raced to her wardrobe. She threw on a dress and a wide-brimmed straw hat. She slipped her feet into her gardening boots. They weren't fancy or frilly. But they were perfect for the kind of day she had planned.

Rosetta flew downstairs and right through the tearoom—in one door and out the open window. When she came out, she had a warm poppy puff roll in each hand.

Soon she was at her favorite breakfast spot in her garden. She settled onto the patch of velvety moss under a large sword fern. The morning sun broke through the overhanging fern fronds. It dappled the ground with pools of light.

"Ahhh," she sighed. "Home, sweet

home." She nibbled on a roll while the song of a nearby warbler danced in her ears. *I haven't been this relaxed in days,* she thought. Even her last lingering worry—that she'd *never* find her style again—didn't matter so much anymore.

After she ate, Rosetta got busy. Lily had taken very good care of everything. But there was plenty to do.

She spent the early morning watering. It was the best time of day for it. "Gives you hours to drink it in," Rosetta cooed at her plants, "before the afternoon sun dries it up."

She weeded through late morning. She moved young sprouts of ivy away from some roses. "You'll have more space to spread out here," she said, putting them at the base of a gray stone wall.

In the early afternoon, she planted. "Rest up," she said to each seedling she tucked into the soil. "Before you know it, you'll be sprouting big and tall!"

Not until late afternoon did Rosetta take a break. "Sweet sunflower seeds!" she exclaimed, noticing the long shadows. She had lost all sense of time. When her stomach rumbled, she realized she had skipped lunch. It was almost dinnertime. But she wasn't ready to leave her garden just yet.

She hopped up onto a toadstool. She felt worn out. She closed her eyes and lay back, her spine curving along the toadstool's top. Her feet and her head hung down over the sides. When she opened her eyes, her garden looked different. It took a wingbeat for her to realize she was seeing it upside down.

At that very moment, a beam of late-afternoon sunlight pierced the trees. The orange light shone through the petal of a peach-colored rose. The petal glowed with fiery warmth. Rosetta gasped. She had never seen such an intense color before. At the same time, the light hit several droplets of water trapped at the base of the petal. The light split into tiny rainbows, stretching between the flower and the ground below.

It was so beautiful, it took Rosetta's breath away.

And to think I sit on this toadstool nearly every day, she said to herself. *I look*

at my garden from this spot all the time! But never like this.

Rosetta felt as if she were seeing her garden for the first time. A wave of pride swelled in her. She had created this wonderful place. She had planted it and tended it, day after day. And now one ray of light had reopened her eyes to its beauty.

Too soon, the moment was gone. The light shifted and the rainbows vanished. The peach rose lost its glow. Rosetta lay there a second longer. The rose was tilting back. Wait! It wasn't the rose. It was her. She felt herself slipping, falling. *Bonk!* She tumbled in a heap to the ground. But a second later, she bounced back up. She was refreshed, revived, and more energetic than she had been all day.

But was it more than just energy? She felt inspired! It was as if there were nothing she couldn't do. Then a pang of disappointment passed through her. *Oh! Why couldn't I have felt this way yesterday? Or the day before? That's when I really needed it.*

She had a funny idea and couldn't help laughing out loud. "Now, if only I had looked at our *crazy dress* upside down . . ." The words nearly bowled her over, like a herd of runaway sprinting thistles. She had an idea. She had a great, clever, original idea.

Just then, she heard voices. They were coming from the climbing-rose arch. "Ro-set-taaaa!" someone was calling.

Speeding over, Rosetta saw Lily and Silvermist flying toward her. "Oh! There you are!" Lily said. A look of concern clouded her face. "How are you?"

"We were worried," said Silvermist. "We haven't seen you all day. And after last night—*whoa!*"

Without stopping, Rosetta grabbed them both by the hand. She pulled them along behind her at breakneck speed.

"Rosetta!" Silvermist had to shout over the sound of air rushing past her ears. "What's the hurry?"

Rosetta shouted back over her shoulder. "The fashion show! We don't have much time! We have to finish our dress!"

Silvermist and Lily looked completely confused.

"What?" Lily asked.

Silvermist shot Lily a concerned look. "The dress is a mess," she said gently. "Don't you remember?"

Rosetta laughed but didn't say another word until they were back in her room.

The dress they had created together still hung from her wardrobe door. "You want to show this in the fashion show?" Silvermist asked, picking it up.

Rosetta held up one finger. "Not this dress, exactly. But maybe it's closer than we thought!"

While Lily and Silvermist watched, Rosetta went to work. She snipped the stitches that held the pieces of the dress together. Then, taking the pieces, she ducked behind a changing screen.

Lily and Silvermist waited patiently. They heard more snipping. They heard rustling fabric. When they heard hammering, they started to worry.

"Rosetta?" called Lily. "Is everything okay?"

"Just . . . about done . . . ," Rosetta called. "Are you ready?" She flew out from behind the screen. She was wearing a completely different dress.

Or was she?

Lily and Silvermist looked closely and saw the pieces they had made. But Lily's colorful top was now the skirt. Silvermist's flowing skirt was now the top. As for Tink's sleeves, Rosetta had taken them apart. She'd linked the copper bangles together into a funky necklace.

"I turned our dress upside down!" Rosetta explained.

"Stormy seas, that's *so* much better!" Silvermist exclaimed.

"It's great!" Lily said. "How in Pixie Hollow did you think of doing that?"

Rosetta smiled and shrugged. "I just got inspired," she said. "Do you think it's good enough for the fashion show?" Even as she asked, she knew the answer.

She didn't doubt herself anymore. It was a beautiful dress, and her fashion sense was back. Still, it made her feel good when both Lily and Silvermist cried, "Yes!"

"But we have to hurry," added Lily, peeking out the window. "The sun! It's almost to the horizon!"

Rosetta zipped to the door. She threw it open and led the way through.

Thwap! A stick swung out into the doorway. It struck Rosetta on the forehead.

Flump! Rosetta dropped like a sack of acorns onto the floor.

10

ROSETTA'S EYES FLUTTERED open again before Silvermist and Lily had finished scolding Tinker Bell.

"She didn't need to be thumped. She was already better!" Lily was saying.

Rosetta waved a hand. "It's okay," she said. "I'm okay. Really." She tried to sit up.

"Wait. Don't rush it," said Silvermist.

But Rosetta insisted. "I have to rush it. Or we'll miss the show!"

Lily and Silvermist looked at each other. They didn't know whether it was a good idea to let Rosetta fly off.

"I know!" said Tink. "Let's test her. Rosetta, what do you think of my dress?"

"Well . . ." Rosetta hesitated for a moment. The others held their breath, waiting for her answer. "I would say . . . make the skirt longer. Add sleeves. And more color, color, color. Or maybe it would be easier to start from scratch?"

Lily, Silvermist, and Tink burst out laughing. "That sounds like the Rosetta we know!" Lily said.

"See?" said Tink. "My plan worked perfectly!"

Now Rosetta laughed, too. "What was I thinking?" she said. "I can't believe I went along with your crazy plan! But we'll talk about that later. Let's get this dress to the fashion show!"

Rosetta jumped to her feet and led the way, racing down the hall. They reached the central stairwell and darted downward. They could hear clapping and cheers from outside. The fashion show was under way!

At the lobby, Rosetta stopped suddenly, causing Tink, Silvermist, and Lily to pile up behind her. Three painting fairies were flying in, each with two open acorn-pots of berry paint. Rosetta zipped to her left to get out of their way.

At the same moment, the first painting

fairy flitted that way, too, dodging Rosetta and her friends. So Rosetta darted to her right—into the path of the second painting fairy! That fairy tried to stop in time. But the third painting fairy was barreling toward her, not watching where she was going.

Over Rosetta's shoulder, Tink saw what was about to happen. "This way!" she cried. She grabbed Rosetta by the hand and yanked her through the open tearoom door. Only then, with Tink and Rosetta out of the way, could Lily and Silvermist see what was heading right for them!

A loud *splat-splatter-splat!* filled the lobby, followed by complete silence. Cautiously, Rosetta and Tink poked

their heads in from the tearoom. Lily and
Silvermist and two of the painting fairies
were covered in bright red berry paint.

Rosetta winced. *Guess Hem took my advice on the paint color after all*, she thought.

"Go on," Lily called to Rosetta and
Tink. "We'll be right there."

Rosetta and Tink flew past the

tearoom. They made a beeline for an open window. But just then, Dulcie came out of the kitchen door to their right. She was carrying a large tiered dessert tray. It was piled high with cream puffs and tarts for after the show.

Tink had no time to react. She crashed into the dessert tray. It flew out of Dulcie's grasp. Tink tumbled through the air and landed with a *squish* on top of a layer of cream puffs.

She wiped whipped cream off her eyelids. She stuck a fingertip in her mouth to taste it. "Yum!" she said. "Don't worry about me, Rosetta! Hurry!"

Rosetta flew on, through the window, into the Home Tree courtyard. The crowd of fairies looked up as she raced overhead. She zipped toward the runway, then ducked backstage. Hem stood there, clipboard in hand.

"Hem!" Rosetta called in a loud whisper. "I'm here! Can I still go on?"

Hem smiled. "You're just in time, Rosetta!" she said. Hem looked her over from head to toe. "And you look beautiful! Wait here! I'll announce you!"

Hem flew out onstage. Rosetta could hear her address the crowd. "We have a dress by a very special guest designer," Hem said. "She's a garden fairy with a passion for fashion. Everybody, give a big hand to . . . Rosetta!"

Two sewing fairies pulled the curtain flaps apart. And the next moments were a lot like Rosetta had imagined they would be. The crowd was clapping. She was flying over the runway, into the center of the courtyard. Every fairy's eyes were on her.

But Rosetta's eyes were on three smiling faces in the crowd. There was Tink, covered in whipped cream. Next to her were paint-drenched Lily and Silvermist. They were clapping and cheering for Rosetta the loudest of all. Rosetta's glow flared brightly. But it wasn't because of pride or excitement. Rosetta was full of gratitude. She had the best friends any fairy could ask for.

Once offstage, she hurried around front and found a seat in the audience. The show wasn't over yet. There were still a few more dresses to see!

Taylor flew out, modeling her cornhusk dress. Then came Tack. Rosetta had to admit the green beads were perfect. Serena finished the show with a dress that was simple and flowing. It looked nothing like a bathrobe.

Now Rosetta was the one clapping and cheering loudest of all. There were so many pretty dresses! Maybe if she asked really, really nicely, Hem would let her borrow one.

Or two.

Or three.

Don't miss any of the magical
Disney Fairies chapter books!

Rosetta's Daring Day

"Oh, what fun!" Rosetta clapped her hands. She pictured herself floating along on a leaf-boat, enjoying the sun as Fawn pointed out the pretty fish that swam below. Of course! That was something they would both enjoy. "Fawn, you're brilliant! You're absolutely—"

Rosetta's words stuck in her throat when Fawn pulled away her blindfold.

Sitting in the water at the bank of the stream were two enormous green bullfrogs. Both were wearing harnesses made of bark rope.

"*Ribbit!*" one of them said.

"We're going frog-riding!" Fawn said with a whoop.